NOVA'S ARK

DAVID KIRK

SCHOLASTIC PRESS

CALLAWAY

NEW YORK

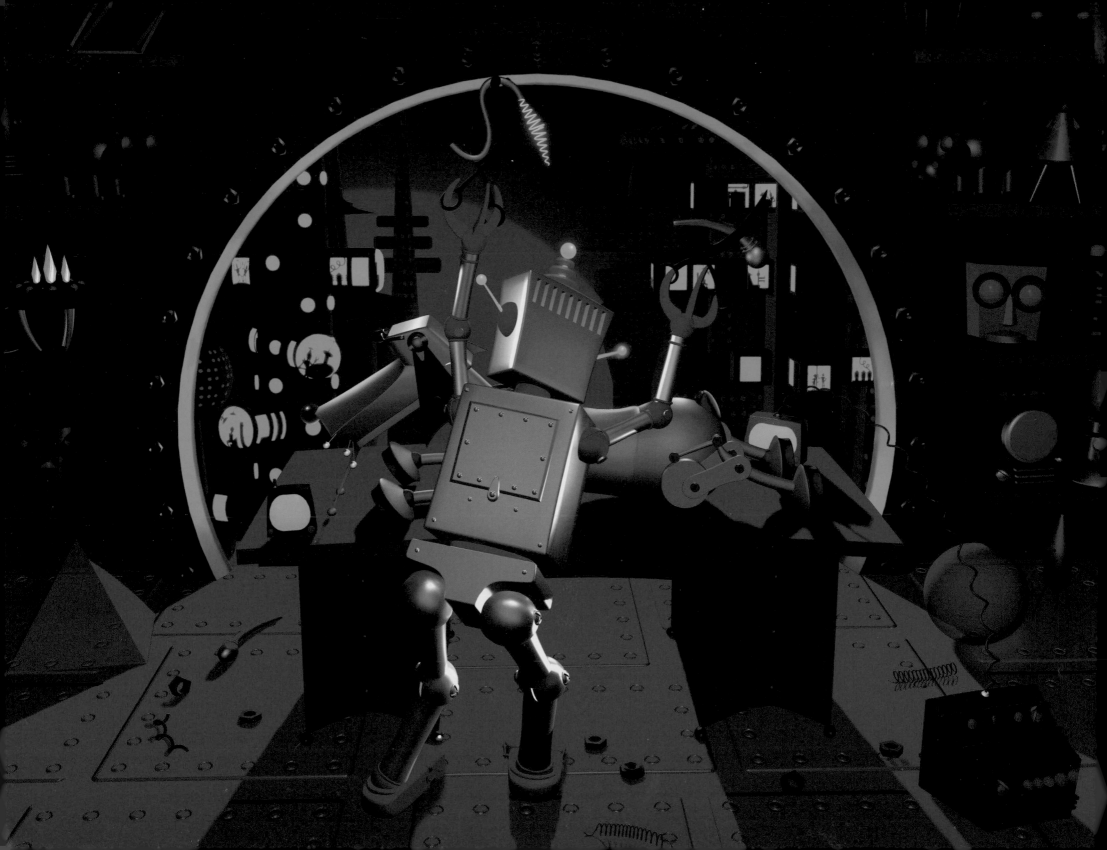

In his tiny bedroom, high above the city, Nova leaned over his workbench — wrapping, twisting, cutting, clipping. The evening sun glinted off his steel brow, then sank behind the crystal spires of Roton, making them glisten like rubies. The stars, visible even during the day, grew bright. Nova tied a pair of copper strands and flicked a switch. His metal dog yipped happily to life, wagging a shiny new wire tail. "Good dog, Sparky," smiled Nova. "Now, let's make a friend for you."

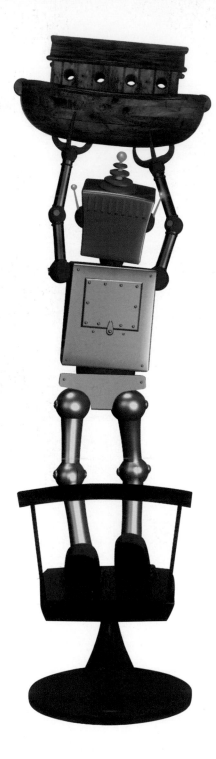

Standing on his chair, Nova stretched to reach the shelf where he kept his most precious possession, a set of wooden animals made in the ancient days of Roton. Carved by men before robots ever existed, the toy had been handed down through a thousand generations of Nova's family. Nearly a year ago, on the night his father, Taspett, had left on his latest space mission, he had passed this treasure on to Nova.

Nova cradled the brittle wooden ark that contained the menagerie. A ship like this one would never fly, he thought, but in those distant times men traveled this planet on seas of water — a liquid that had vanished from Roton long ago. He carefully removed the animals from the ark, turning special attention to a tiny lion. "What do you think, Sparky?" he asked. "A cat for you to play with?"

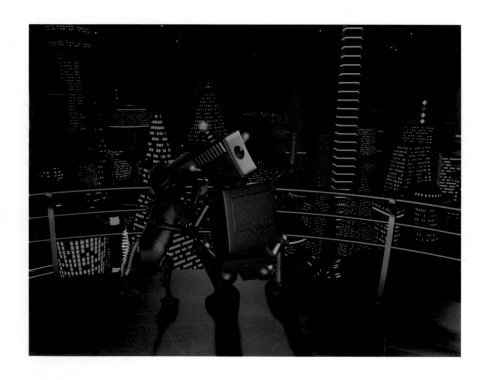

O utside his window, a shooting star drew Nova's attention. From his balcony, he gazed at the twilight, raising a steel hand to a glimmering star in the western sky. "Dad's supposed to be near that one," he sighed. "Don't worry, Sparky, he'll be home soon."

His mother, Luna, was stirring oil broth when Nova entered the kitchen. As they sat down to their steaming bowls, Nova loaded a post disc into the holograph player. Taspett appeared within the swirling green light. Grinning excitedly, he lifted a piece of glowing crystal toward the camera. The grinding engines of a huge mining machine nearly drowned out his shout: "I'LL BE HOME SOON!" But this disc had come months ago. He had been assigned to continue his search for crystal. On this planet of robots, crystal energy was essential to life, and there was never enough to go around.

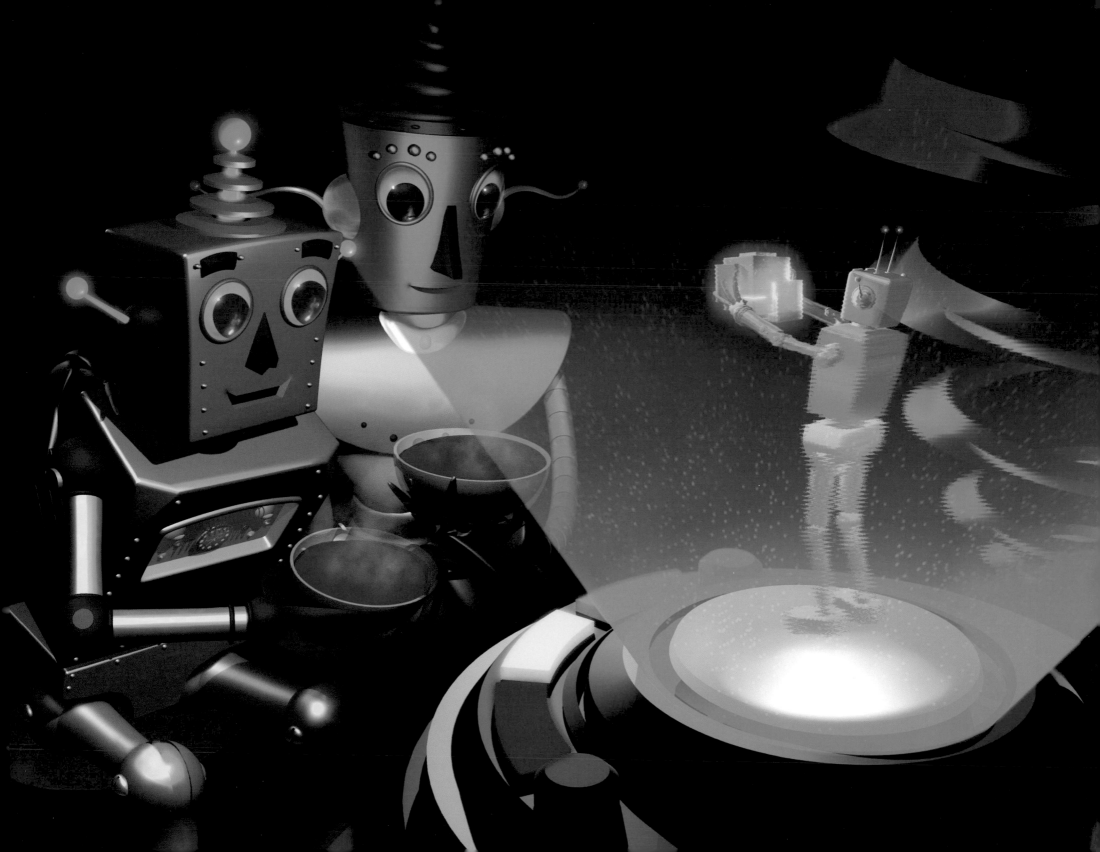

After dinner, Nova studied a disc on starship design. It wasn't meant for little boys; still, he knew it by heart. He believed that if he just tried hard enough, he could be the youngest star pilot ever. Perhaps he would be the one to find Zyte, the mythic moon of light. His mother laughed at the idea, but Nova knew better. In a thousand bedtime stories, his dad had told him of this magical hidden sphere — a source of crystal energy so powerful and abundant that it could fuel Roton forever. Deep among the stars, it waited — waited for him. His sleep mode auto-initiating, Nova's eyes went blurry as he scanned the screen. No longer able to focus, he plugged himself into the dream console. He dreamt of flying to the stars — flying with his dad.

The glass skytowers of Roton glowed pink, reflecting the faint morning sun. Eyes flickering, Nova sprang from his sleep platform and quickly performed his morning oiling. This was a day he had been anticipating for months — the class field trip to Axion, Roton's greatest Space Center. He packed a case with his best model spaceships and gulped down his breakfast lube-pack whole. His mother clanked his steel cheek with a kiss as he rushed out the door.

At school, Nova showed off the models he had built to his classmates. His girlfriend, Elix, was nearly as excited as Nova. If only class could be like this every day!

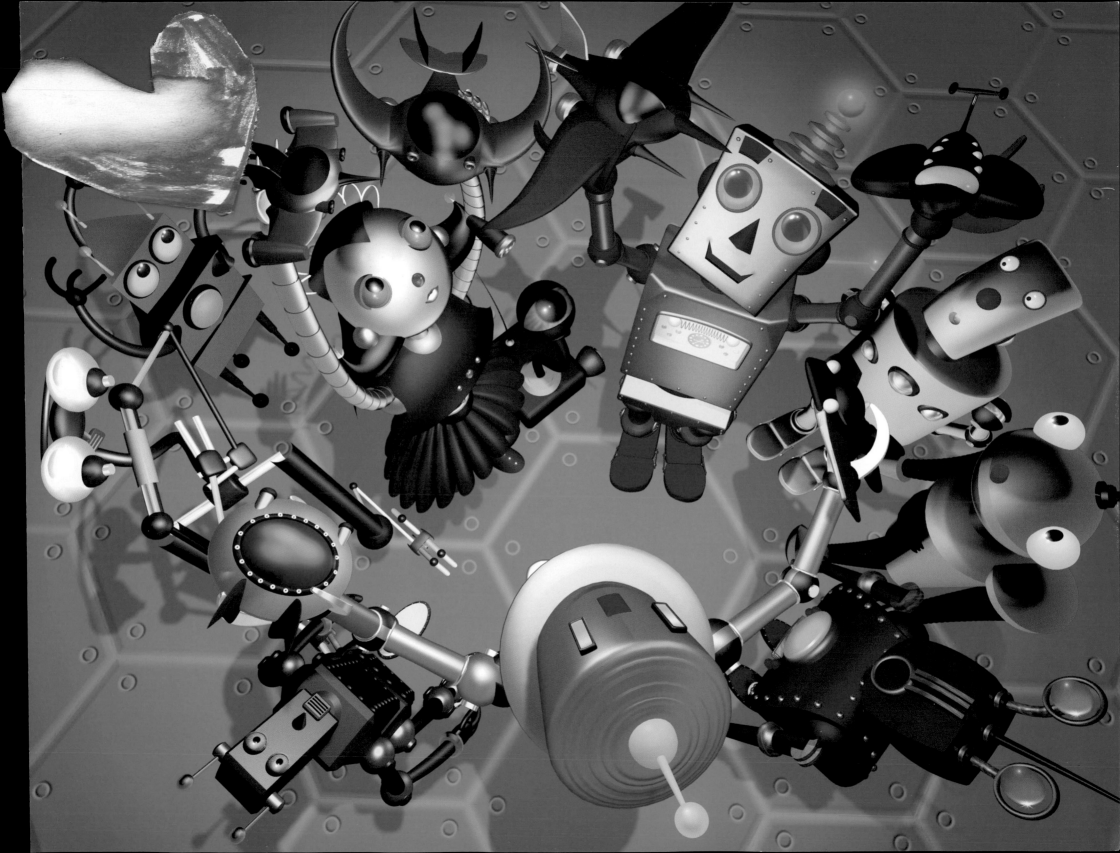

The Space Center was the most glorious place Nova had ever seen. It was miles high and miles across. Everywhere Nova looked, strange and beautiful ships took off to exotic worlds. As the highlight of the tour, each child was allowed to sit behind the console of a real Glax Cruiser. When it was Nova's turn, his teacher, Mrs. Vettik, laughed, "That's the proper place for you, Nova. Someday you'll fly into space like your father. Exploration is in your wiring!"

On the roof of the Space Center, Nova squirmed uncomfortably as he waited for the hover bus with his classmates. All around him, majestic ships blasted into space, but here he was, as always, going nowhere. Just below him, the nose of that Glax Cruiser poked temptingly over its launch pad. "What's the harm in another look?" he thought, slipping quietly out of line.

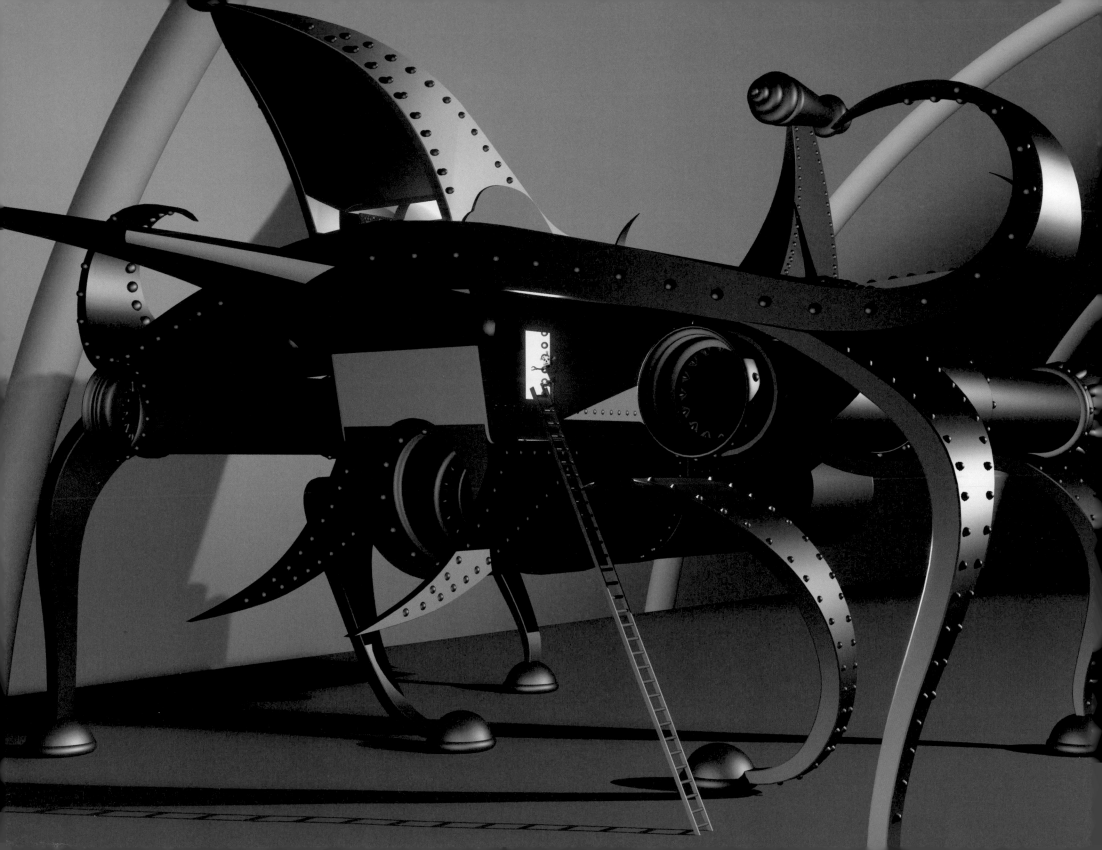

T he hangar was empty when Nova stepped through the hatch of the Glax Cruiser. At the pilot's console, he ran his hands over the gleaming controls.

"Dad stands here when he's taking off," he whispered. His teacher's words echoed in his head: "Exploration is in your wiring!" Panel lights flashed, leading his eye to a luminous red lever. Nova stared, knowing very well that he shouldn't touch it. But, almost involuntarily, his arm raised. It was just as though he was watching somebody else's hand pull the lever firmly down.

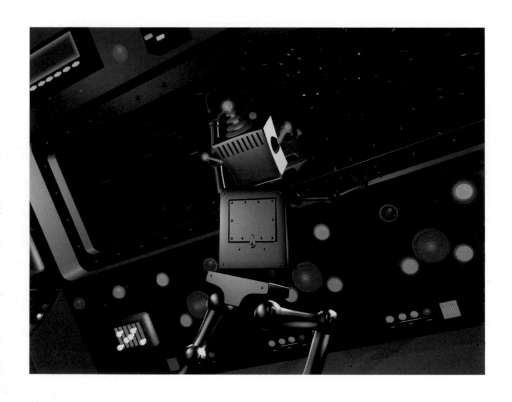

Nova was thrown to the floor as the spaceship roared to life. Terrified, he struggled to his feet and peered out of the view port. His planet shrank to a speck as the cruiser rocketed away. Then Roton was gone. Nova was lost and alone in empty space.

For many days he drifted among the stars, afraid to touch the controls again. Somebody will come and find me, he thought. But as the weeks passed, he realized that he might never be found. "Then I'll learn to fly the ship," he said to himself. The controls were complex. Even though he had studied spaceships, the cruiser wouldn't always do what he wanted. But it wasn't long before he got the hang of it, and even enjoyed buzzing around the planets.

For months Nova searched for home. His ship was nearly out of fuel. He tried to land on the golden moon of a gaseous planet, but in its strong gravity, he lost power. The ship went haywire. It spun. It flipped. It nearly shook to pieces, but Nova held on. It was scary, but felt great, too — slicing through the mountainous clouds. But ahead — "That's not a mountainous cloud," he gasped. "IT'S A MOUNTAIN!" Nova pulled hard on the wheel, but the ship wouldn't lift. It slammed into the slope. He felt a great lurch as the engine exploded, blowing the ship down the mountainside like a ball from a cannon.

For miles it jarred and bumped over the rocks. Then, gliding onto a sandy plain, it came gently to rest. Nova pried the door open and stepped out into a new world.

21

Climbing to a high ledge, Nova gazed across the barren rocks of this desolate moon. There were no signs of robot life. How would he ever get home? Who would take care of his mother? Who would take care of Sparky? All his life he'd wanted to explore new worlds, but now that he had the chance, he was miserable. "Is this how my father feels when he's away?" Nova wondered as he sank into sleep.

The glint of a familiar curl of wire was the first thing to meet Nova's eyes when he woke to a cheerful new sun. It gave him an idea. He knew that his ship would never fly again, so he took out his tools and snipped the wire. Then he took other parts from the ship's engine and computers. He worked for days. Finally he was finished. "Nice to meet you," barked Sparky #2.

After that, Nova built many animals from pieces of his large ship. He modeled them after those in his ancient wooden ark. First came the lion, then the giraffe. The penguin and the hedgehog were next, followed by an iguana, a mule, a deer, a buzzard, a spider, a turkey, a monkey, a bat, a cat, a hummingbird, a kangaroo, and a cockatoo.

Nova had a good eye for detail, but he couldn't always remember which animal was supposed to be bigger — "Was a mouse bigger than a moose?" he asked himself.

Lastly, with the hull, and nearly all the remaining parts of his ship, he constructed a truly wondrous animal — an elephant ark, whose mighty trunk bellowed a message deep into the heavens: "HELP!"

Surely my dad will find me now, thought Nova. He bowed low before his most magnificent creation. "Your name will be Trumpet," he declared proudly.

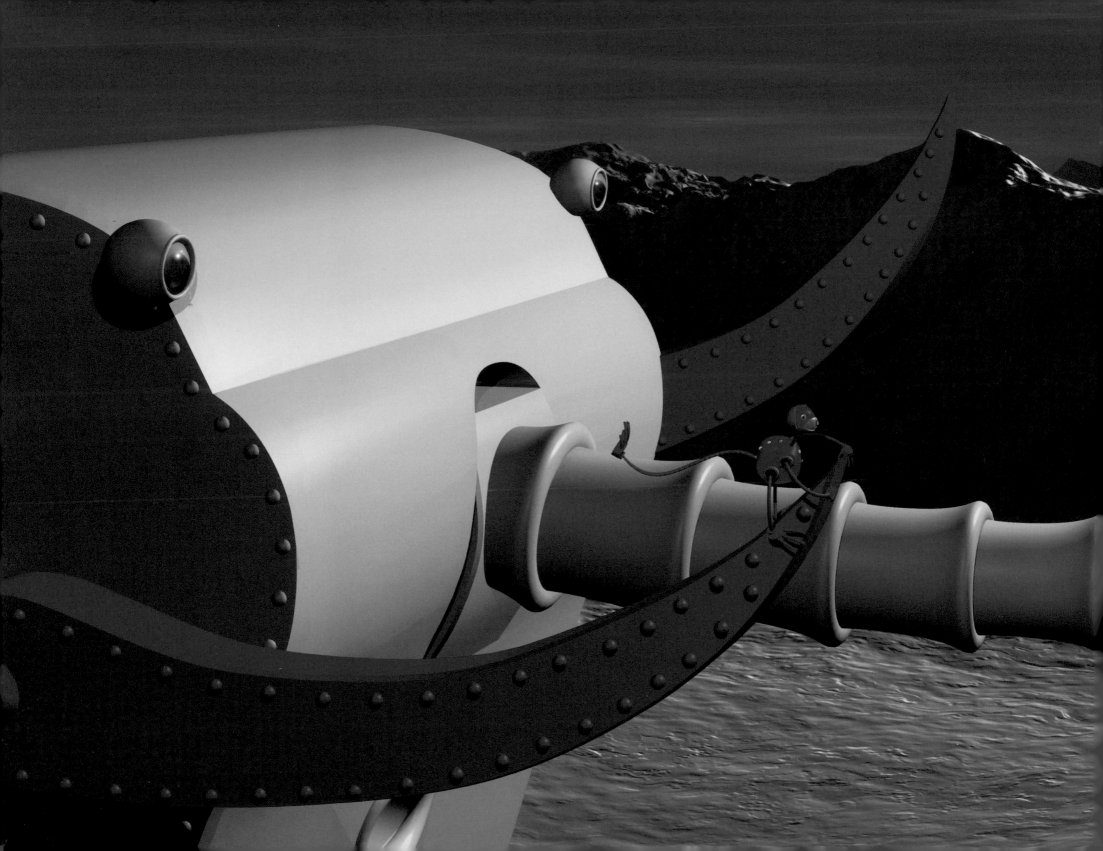

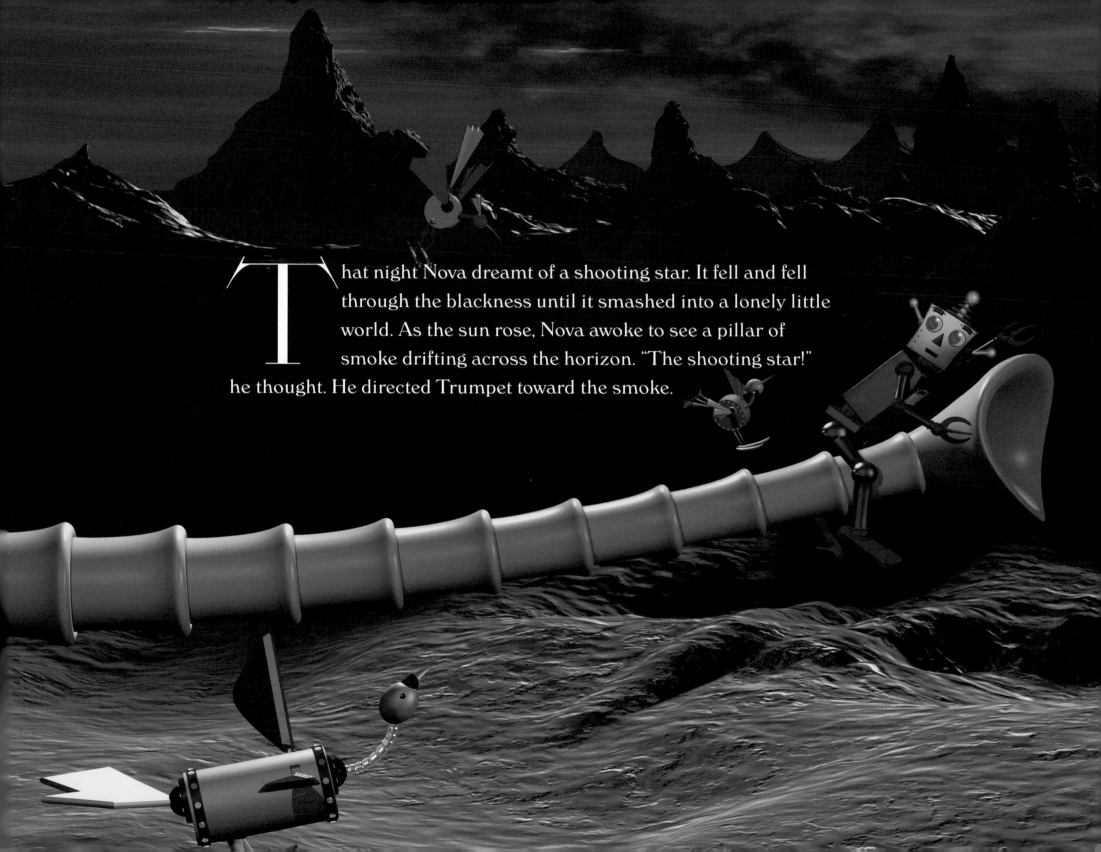

That night Nova dreamt of a shooting star. It fell and fell through the blackness until it smashed into a lonely little world. As the sun rose, Nova awoke to see a pillar of smoke drifting across the horizon. "The shooting star!" he thought. He directed Trumpet toward the smoke.

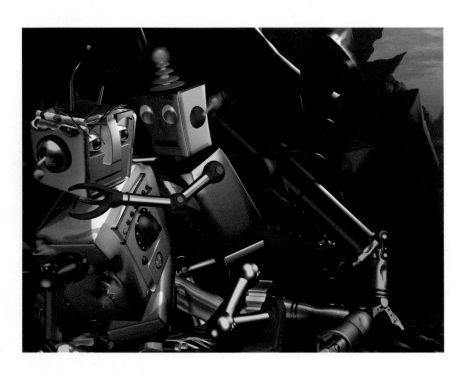

I t's a fallen spaceship!" Nova cried. Twisted wreckage was scattered as far as he could see. The robot pilot lay ripped to pieces in the sand. "Dad!" shouted Nova.

Taspett's eyes flickered as he struggled to consciousness. "Nova," he coughed, "I thought I'd never find you!" Then the light faded from his eyes.

Though he worked for days, never stopping to rest, Nova couldn't revive his father. Exhausted, he sobbed in despair.

His animals stood quietly around him. Trumpet broke the silence. "I've often thought of my trunk as very much like an arm," he said. "If it would help your father, I'd like you to take any part of it you need."

"And a tail is a wondrous instrument," said Sparky #2. "I'm sure your father would like to have my tail!"

Each animal gave something of himself for Nova's father. Inspired by their sacrifice, Nova gave the greatest gift of all — a valve from his very heart.

Their generosity was rewarded. "I feel like a new robot!" said Taspett — leaping to his kangaroo feet and swishing his shiny new tail. The proud father looked down at the strange and wonderful body Nova had built for him.

"My brilliant son!" he laughed, lifting his boy into the air. "My Nova!"

Together, father and son looked to see what they could do about Taspett's wrecked ship. The hull was broken beyond repair, but the engine was still intact. "The engine is no use without a spaceship," said Taspett sadly. But Nova had an idea. With Trumpet's help, they dragged the huge engine from the crater it had carved. It was then that Nova and his father made the discovery of their lives — a gaping hole at the bottom of the crater revealed a giant cavern of dazzling crystal. Taspett stood in awe, shielding his eyes against the blinding light. "You've found what I've been searching for all these years!" he roared. "We're on Zyte!"

34

N ova and his animals attached the engine to Trumpet's belly. They all loaded his fuel tank with the radiant Zyte crystals, then gathered more and filled his hull. "Time to head home!" smiled Taspett.

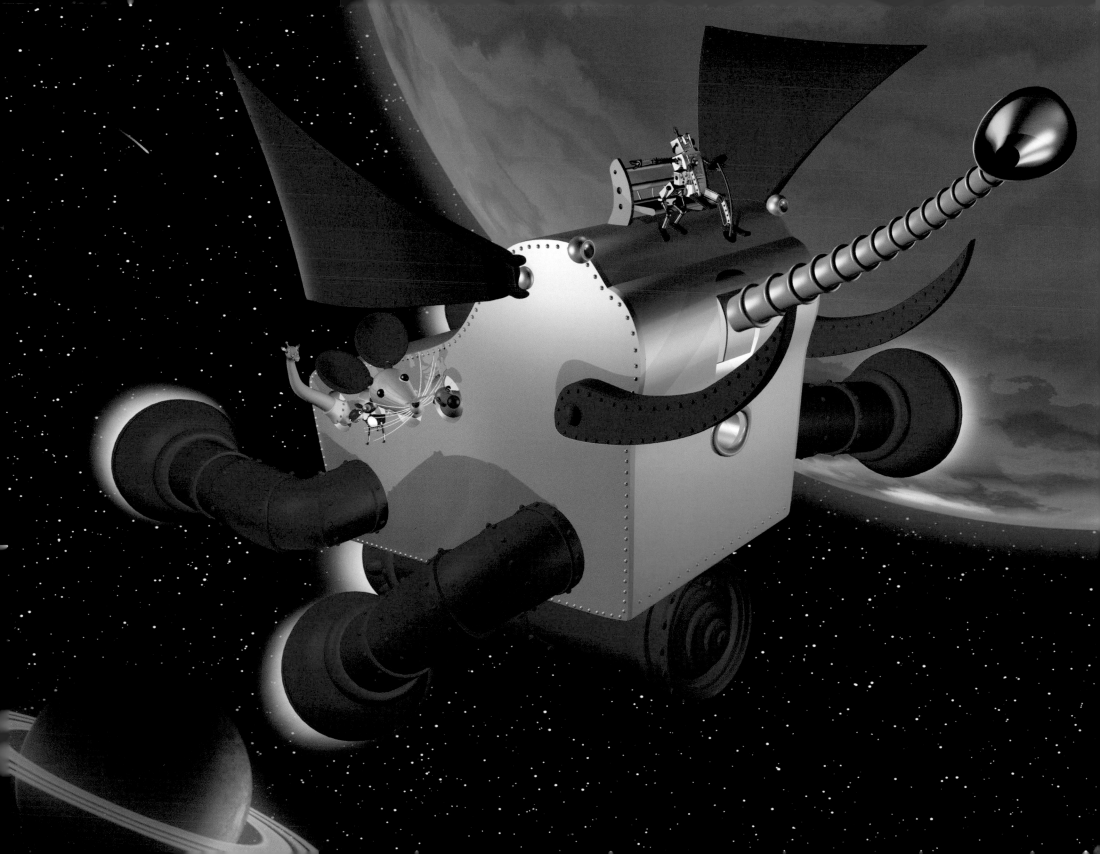

Back on Roton, Nova was a great hero. There was enough Zyte crystal to power their world forever. Luna was overjoyed: Her husband and son were home for good. Taspett was happy to give up searching the galaxies for energy. "It was really a very lonely job," he said.

From then on, when Nova's father wanted to explore exotic planets, he made sure the whole family came along.